Classic

F
Hilton, J.
Good-bye, Mr. Ch

D0464952

GOOD-BYE, MR. CHIPS

"Good-bye Mr Chips"

Good-bye, MR. CHIPS

BY
James Hilton

Illustrations by H.M.BROCK

AN ATLANTIC MONTHLY PRESS BOOK
LITTLE, BROWN AND COMPANY

7

Hilton, J.

Thirieth Printing

ATLANTIC—LITTLE, BROWN BOOKS
ARE PUBLISHED BY
LITTLE, BROWN AND COMPANY
IN ASSOCIATION WITH
THE ATLANTIC MONTHLY PRESS

BP

*Published simultaneously in Canada
by Little, Brown & Company (Canada) Limited*

PRINTED IN THE UNITED STATES OF AMERICA

122043

FOREWORD

James Hilton was not only a very good novelist, he was a very good talker. Though he was English-born, he lived for the latter part of his life in California, and on my visits to the Coast I always looked forward to having a leisurely dinner with him, in the course of which we would compare notes about everything under the sun. I remember well our last meeting, for it occurred shortly after we had learned for sure that the Russians had perfected, far ahead of schedule, their atomic bomb. Jimmie was depressed by the news, for in his farsighted way he saw at once that this would involve us in the most dangerous armament race in human history.

I knew that he was at work on a new novel and at a favorable opening I asked how it was going.

FOREWORD

"I have made four beginnings," he said. "I think I have got a good idea and for about a week I'll start off each morning at the typewriter with a feeling of confidence. And then just after I have passed page fifty, it is as if the words 'So what!' suddenly stood out in capitals on the page. We haven't got the confidence we once had, now that we know about those bombs. It is a hard time in which to try to write fiction."

Good-bye, Mr. Chips, Hilton's most successful novel, and surely the most endearing portrait of a schoolteacher in our time, was written in another kind of desperation. In November, 1933, James Hilton was struggling to meet his deadline for a story for the Christmas issue of the *British Weekly.* He needed the fifty pounds (then two hundred and fifty dollars) he would be paid for the story; and he hadn't an idea. After a sleepless night, he rose and went for a bicycle ride in the foggy dawn. When he returned, ravenous, for

vi

breakfast he had his lead, and *Mr. Chips* was written in longhand and almost without alteration in the four days that followed. It was published with little notice in London, but when it appeared in the *Atlantic* the following April, the American acclaim woke up the English. Everywhere you went you heard people talking about Mr. Chips as if he were someone they had known. Bishop William A. Lawrence spoke of *Mr. Chips* in a sermon at Trinity Church in Boston; William Lyon Phelps, the most quoted professor in New Haven, said it was "a masterpiece and ought to be so regarded a hundred years from now"; and Alexander Woollcott, who as the Town Crier had a more stimulating effect on readers at that period than any other single person, devoted a whole broadcast to *Mr. Chips,* which he called "the most profoundly moving story that has passed this way in several years."

To Jimmie Hilton the theme was as natural as

breathing. His father was a headmaster, and at the boarding school where Jimmie was sent, he was happy. Had he cared more for athletics he might have been less observant of his teachers. But he was a roly-poly, good tempered, and no good at games. His mind was inquiring and responsive: he wrote poems about the Russian Revolution and the sinking of the *Lusitania,* and broke all speed records for reciting the long Latin grace.

Mr. Chips, as Hilton drew him, is a composite; he has the wise and sweetening influence of Jimmie's father, the discipline and idiosyncrasy of his Latin teacher, and the unsparing devotion which the profession demands of all. And this was why people wrote him from all parts of the globe to say that they had been taught by the original Mr. Chips. He was thirty-three when he wrote this story, but it established him for life.

EDWARD WEEKS

PREFACE

Good-bye, Mr. Chips was written in London during a foggy week of November, 1933. I am chary of using the word "inspiration," which is too often something nonexistent that a writer waits for when he is lazy; but, as a matter of record, *Good-bye, Mr. Chips* was written more quickly, more easily, and with fewer subsequent alterations than anything I had ever written before, or have ever written since.

It was first published in the Christmas number of the *British Weekly,* in December 1933; after which, with a certain wild abandon, I had it sent to the *Atlantic Monthly* — a magazine which I had long held as a secret pinnacle of ambition. The *Atlantic* printed the story in its

issue of April 1934, and about the same time pro-
posed its publication as a book. This publication took place on June 8. Four months later
Good-bye, Mr. Chips first appeared as a book
in England, from Messrs. Hodder and Stoughton.
Thus one may summarize that, having been
written and first printed in its native land, it
was discovered by America, and later came back
to England with the success that America had
given it. And now, again in America, it appears
in this new and sumptuous dress.

If I recount these details with pride, I do so
also with modesty, for I know how few are the
writers to whom such romances happen, and
that, with no matter how much or little merit,
a portion of luck must be distilled. But I do
take pride in the reception that America has
given to my very English book; certainly no
author could ever have enjoyed his correspond-
ence more than I have during the past year. One

feature has been the discovery of the original
Mr. Chips in so many different parts of the
world; and I believe those letters from readers
have told the whole truth, and that my tribute
to a great profession has fitted a great many
members of it everywhere.

J. H.

WANSTEAD, LONDON
March 1935

ILLUSTRATIONS

GOOD-BYE, MR. CHIPS

WHEN you are getting on in years (but not ill, of course), you get very sleepy at times, and the hours seem to pass like lazy cattle moving across a landscape. It was like that for Chips as the autumn term progressed and the days shortened till it was actually dark enough to light the gas before call-over. For Chips, like some old sea captain, still measured time by the signals of the past; and well he might, for he lived at Mrs. Wickett's, just across the road from the School.

3

He had been there more than a decade, ever since he finally gave up his mastership; and it was Brookfield far more than Greenwich time that both he and his landlady kept. "Mrs. Wickett," Chips would sing out, in that jerky, high-pitched voice that had still a good deal of sprightliness in it, "you might bring me a cup of tea before prep, will you?"

When you are getting on in years it is nice to sit by the fire and drink a cup of tea and listen to the school bell sounding dinner, call-over, prep, and lights-out. Chips always wound up the clock after that last bell; then he put the wire guard in front of the fire, turned out the gas, and carried a detective novel to bed. Rarely did he read more than a page of it before sleep came swiftly and peacefully, more like a mystic intensifying of perception than any changeful entrance into another world. For his days and nights were equally full of dreaming.

4

He was getting on in years (but not ill, of course); indeed, as Doctor Merivale said, there was really nothing the matter with him. "My dear fellow, you're fitter than I am," Merivale would say, sipping a glass of sherry when he called every fortnight or so. "You're past the age when people get these horrible diseases; you're one of the few lucky ones who're going to die a really natural death. That is, of course, if you die at all. You're such a remarkable old boy that one never knows." But when Chips had a cold or when east winds roared over the fenlands, Merivale would sometimes take Mrs. Wickett aside in the lobby and whisper: "Look after him, you know. His chest . . . it puts a strain on his heart. Nothing really wrong with him — only anno domini, but that's the most fatal complaint of all, in the end."

Anno domini . . . by Jove, yes. Born in 1848, and taken to the Great Exhibition as a toddling child — not many people still alive could boast a thing like that. Besides, Chips could even remember Brookfield in Wetherby's time. A phenomenon, that was. Wetherby had been an old man in those days — 1870 — easy to remember because of the Franco-Prussian War. Chips had put in for Brookfield after a year at Melbury, which he had n't liked, because he had been ragged there a good deal. But Brookfield he *had* liked, almost from the beginning. He remembered that day of his preliminary interview — sunny June, with the air full of flower scents and the plick-plock of cricket on the pitch. Brookfield was playing Barnhurst, and one of the Barnhurst boys, a chubby little fellow, made a brilliant century. Queer that a thing like that should stay in the memory so clearly. Wetherby himself was very fatherly and courteous; he must have been ill then, poor chap, for he died during the summer vacation, before Chips began his first term. But the two had seen and spoken to each other, anyway.

Chips often thought, as he sat by the fire at Mrs. Wickett's: I am probably the only man in the world who has a vivid recollection of old Wetherby. . . . Vivid, yes; it was a frequent picture in his mind, that summer day with the sunlight filtering through the dust in Wetherby's study. "You are a young man, Mr. Chipping, and Brookfield is an old foundation. Youth and age often combine well. Give your enthusiasm to Brookfield, and Brookfield will give you something in return. And don't let anyone play tricks with you. I — er — gather that discipline was not always your strong point at Melbury?"

"Well, no, perhaps not, sir."

"Never mind; you 're full young; it 's largely a matter of experience. You have another chance here. Take up a firm attitude from the beginning — that 's the secret of it."

7

Perhaps it was. He remembered that first tremendous ordeal of taking prep; a September sunset more than half a century ago; Big Hall full of lusty barbarians ready to pounce on him as their legitimate prey. His youth, fresh-complexioned, high-collared, and side-whiskered (odd fashions people followed in those days), at the mercy of five hundred unprincipled ruffians to whom the baiting of new masters was a fine art, an exciting sport, and something of a tradition. Decent little beggars individually, but, as a mob, just pitiless and implacable. The sudden hush as he took his place at the desk on the dais; the scowl he assumed to cover his inward nervousness; the tall clock ticking behind him, and the smells of ink and varnish; the last blood-red rays slanting in slabs through the stained-glass windows. Someone dropped a desk lid. Quickly, he must take everyone by surprise; he must show that there was no nonsense about him. "You there in the fifth row — you with the red hair — what's your name?" "Colley, sir." "Very well, Colley, you have a hundred lines." No trouble at all after that. He had won his first round.

And years later, when Colley was an alderman of the City of London and a baronet and various other things, he sent his son (also red-haired) to Brookfield, and Chips would say: "Colley, your father was the first boy I ever punished when I came here twenty-five years ago. He deserved it then, and you deserve it now." How they all laughed; and how Sir Richard laughed when his son wrote home the story in next Sunday's letter!

And again, years after that, many years after that, there was an even better joke. For another Colley had just arrived — son of the Colley who was a son of the first Colley. And Chips would say, punctuating his remarks with that little "umph-um" that had by then become a habit with him: "Colley, you are — umph — a splendid example of — umph — inherited traditions. I remember your grandfather — umph — he could never grasp the Ablative Absolute. A stupid fellow, your grandfather. And your father, too — umph — I remember him — he used to sit at that far desk by the wall — he was n't much better, either. But I do believe — my dear Colley — that you are — umph — the biggest fool of the lot!" Roars of laughter.

A great joke, this growing old — but a sad joke, too, in a way. And as Chips sat by his fire with autumn gales rattling the windows, the waves of humor and sadness swept over him very often until tears fell, so that when Mrs. Wickett came in with his cup of tea she did not know whether he had been laughing or crying. And neither did Chips himself.

II

Across the road behind a rampart of ancient elms
lay Brookfield, russet under its autumn mantle of
creeper. A group of eighteenth-century build-
ings centred upon a quadrangle, and there were
acres of playing fields beyond; then came the
small dependent village and the open fen country. Brookfield, as Wetherby had said, was an
old foundation; established in the reign of Elizabeth, as a grammar school, it might, with better
luck, have become as famous as Harrow. Its

11

luck, however, had been not so good; the School went up and down, dwindling almost to non-existence at one time, becoming almost illustrious at another. It was during one of these latter periods, in the reign of the first George, that the main structure had been rebuilt and large additions made. Later, after the Napoleonic Wars and until mid-Victorian days, the School declined again, both in numbers and in repute. Wetherby, who came in 1840, restored its fortunes somewhat; but its subsequent history never raised it to front-rank status. It was, nevertheless, a good school of the second rank. Several notable families supported it; it supplied fair samples of the history-making men of the age — judges, members of parliament, colonial administrators, a few peers and bishops. Mostly, however, it turned out merchants, manufacturers, and professional men, with a good sprinkling of country squires and parsons. It was the sort of school

12

which, when mentioned, would sometimes make snobbish people confess that they rather thought they had heard of it.

But if it had not been this sort of school it would probably not have taken Chips. For Chips, in any social or academic sense, was just as respectable, but no more brilliant, than Brookfield itself.

It had taken him some time to realize this, at the beginning. Not that he was boastful or conceited, but he had been, in his early twenties, as ambitious as most other young men at such an age. His dream had been to get a headship eventually, or at any rate a senior mastership in a really first-class school; it was only gradually, after repeated trials and failures, that he realized the inadequacy of his qualifications. His degree, for instance, was not particularly good, and his discipline, though good enough and improving, was not absolutely reliable under all conditions.

He had no private means and no family connections of any importance. About 1880, after he had been at Brookfield a decade, he began to recognize that the odds were heavily against his being able to better himself by moving elsewhere; but about that time, also, the possibility of staying where he was began to fill a comfortable niche in his mind. At forty, he was rooted, settled, and quite happy. At fifty, he was the doyen of the staff. At sixty, under a new and youthful Head, he *was* Brookfield — the guest of honor at Old Brookfeldian dinners, the court of appeal in all matters affecting Brookfield history and traditions. And in 1913, when he turned sixty-five, he retired, was presented with a check and a writing desk and a clock, and went across the road to live at Mrs. Wickett's. A decent career, decently closed; three cheers for old Chips, they all shouted, at that uproarious end-of-term dinner.

Three cheers, indeed; but there was more to come, an unguessed epilogue, an encore played to a tragic audience.

I⊤ was a small but very comfortable and sunny room that Mrs. Wickett let to him. The house itself was ugly and pretentious; but that did n't matter. It was convenient — that was the main thing. For he liked, if the weather were mild enough, to stroll across to the playing fields in an afternoon and watch the games. He liked to smile and exchange a few words with the boys when they touched their caps to him. He made a special point of getting to know all the new

boys and having them to tea with him during
their first term. He always ordered a walnut
cake with pink icing from Reddaway's, in the
village, and during the winter term there were
crumpets, too — a little pile of them in front of
the fire, soaked in butter so that the bottom one
lay in a little shallow pool. His guests found it
fun to watch him make tea — mixing careful
spoonfuls from different caddies. And he would
ask the new boys where they lived, and if they
had family connections at Brookfield. He kept
watch to see that their plates were never empty,
and punctually at five, after the session had lasted
an hour, he would glance at the clock and say:
"Well — umph — it's been very delightful —
umph — meeting you like this — I'm sorry —
umph — you can't stay. . . ." And he would
smile and shake hands with them in the porch,
leaving them to race across the road to the
School with their comments. "Decent old boy,

Chips. Gives you a jolly good tea, anyhow, and you *do* know when he wants you to push off. . . ."

And Chips also would be making his comments — to Mrs. Wickett when she entered his room to clear away the remains of the party. "A most — umph — interesting time, Mrs. Wickett. Young Branksome tells me — umph — that his uncle was Major Collingwood — the Collingwood we had here in — umph — nought-two, I think it was. Dear me, I remember Collingwood very well. I once thrashed him — umph — for climbing on to the gymnasium roof — to get a ball out of the gutter. Might have — umph — broken his neck, the young fool. Do you remember him, Mrs. Wickett? He must have been in your time."

Mrs. Wickett, before she saved money, had been in charge of the linen room at the School.

"Yes, I knew 'im, sir. Cheeky, 'e was to me, gener'ly. But we never 'ad no bad words between us. Just cheeky-like. 'E never meant no harm. That kind never does, sir. Was n't it 'im that got the medal, sir?"

"Yes, a D.S.O."

"Will you be wanting anything else, sir?"

"Nothing more now — umph — till chapel time. He was killed — in Egypt, I think. . . . Yes — umph — you can bring my supper about then."

"Very good, sir."

A pleasant, placid life, at Mrs. Wickett's. He had no worries; his pension was adequate, and there was a little money saved up besides. He could afford everything and anything he wanted. His room was furnished simply and with schoolmasterly taste: a few bookshelves and sporting trophies; a mantelpiece crowded with fixture cards and signed photographs of boys and men;

a worn Turkey carpet; big easy-chairs; pictures on the wall of the Acropolis and the Forum. Nearly everything had come out of his old house-master's room in School House. The books were chiefly classical, the classics having been his subject; there was, however, a seasoning of history and belles-lettres. There was also a bottom shelf piled up with cheap editions of detective novels. Chips enjoyed these. Sometimes he took down Vergil or Xenophon and read for a few moments, but he was soon back again with Doctor Thorn-dyke or Inspector French. He was not, despite his long years of assiduous teaching, a very profound classical scholar; indeed, he thought of Latin and Greek far more as dead languages from which English gentlemen ought to know a few quotations than as living tongues that had ever been spoken by living people. He liked those short leading articles in the *Times* that introduced a few tags that he recognized. To be among the

20

dwindling number of people who understood such things was to him a kind of secret and valued freemasonry; it represented, he felt, one of the chief benefits to be derived from a classical education.

So there he lived, at Mrs. Wickett's, with his quiet enjoyments of reading and talking and re-membering; an old man, white-haired and only a little bald, still fairly active for his years, drinking tea, receiving callers, busying himself with corrections for the next edition of the Brook-feldian Directory, writing his occasional letters in thin, spidery, but very legible script. He had new masters to tea, as well as new boys. There were two of them that autumn term, and as they were leaving after their visit one of them com-mented: "Quite a character, the old boy, isn't he? All that fuss about mixing the tea — a typical bachelor, if ever there was one."

Which was oddly incorrect; because Chips was

not a bachelor at all. He had married; though it was so long ago that none of the staff at Brookfield could remember his wife.

IV

THERE came to him, stirred by the warmth of the fire and the gentle aroma of tea, a thousand tangled recollections of old times. Spring — the spring of 1896. He was forty-eight — an age at which a permanence of habits begins to be predictable. He had just been appointed house-master; with this and his classical forms, he had made for himself a warm and busy corner of life. During the summer vacation he went up to the Lake District with Rowden, a colleague; they walked and climbed for a week, until Rowden had to leave suddenly on some family business. Chips stayed on alone at Wasdale Head, where he boarded in a small farmhouse.

One day, climbing on Great Gable, he noticed a girl waving excitedly from a dangerous-looking ledge. Thinking she was in difficulties, he hastened toward her, but in doing so slipped himself and wrenched his ankle. As it turned out, she was not in difficulties at all, but was merely signaling to a friend farther down the mountain; she was an expert climber, better even than Chips, who was pretty good. Thus he found himself the rescued instead of the rescuer; and neither rôle was one for which he had much relish. For he did not, he would have said, care for women; he never felt at home or at ease with them; and that monstrous creature beginning to be talked about, the New Woman of the nineties, filled him with horror. He was a quiet, conventional

24

He noticed
a girl waving

person, and the world, viewed from the haven of Brookfield, seemed to him full of distasteful innovations; there was a fellow named Bernard Shaw who had the strangest and most reprehensible opinions; there was Ibsen, too, with his disturbing plays; and there was this new craze for bicycling which was being taken up by women equally with men. Chips did not hold with all this modern newness and freedom. He had a vague notion, if he ever formulated it, that nice women were weak, timid, and delicate, and that nice men treated them with a polite but rather distant chivalry. He had not, therefore, expected to find a woman on Great Gable; but, having encountered one who seemed to need masculine help, it was even more terrifying that she should turn the tables by helping him. For she did. She and her friend had to. He could scarcely walk, and it was a hard job getting him down the steep track to Wasdale.

Her name was Katherine Bridges; she was twenty-five — young enough to be Chips's daughter. She had blue, flashing eyes and freckled cheeks and smooth straw-colored hair. She too was staying at a farm, on holiday with a girl friend, and as she considered herself responsible for Chips's accident, she used to bicycle along the side of the lake to the house in which the quiet, middle-aged, serious-looking man lay resting.

That was how she thought of him at first. And he, because she rode a bicycle and was un-afraid to visit a man alone in a farmhouse sitting room, wondered vaguely what the world was coming to. His sprain put him at her mercy, and it was soon revealed to him how much he might need that mercy. She was a governess out of a job, with a little money saved up; she read and admired Ibsen; she believed that women ought to be admitted to the universities; she even thought they ought to have a vote. In politics

28

she was a radical, with leanings toward the views
of people like Bernard Shaw and William Morris.
All her ideas and opinions she poured out to
Chips during those summer afternoons at Wasdale Head; and he, because he was not very
articulate, did not at first think it worth while to
contradict them. Her friend went away, but she
stayed; what *could* you do with such a person,
Chips thought. He used to hobble with sticks
along a footpath leading to the tiny church; there
was a stone slab on the wall, and it was comfortable to sit down, facing the sunlight and the
green-brown majesty of the Gable and listening
to the chatter of — well, yes, Chips had to admit
it — a very beautiful girl.

He had never met anyone like her. He had
always thought that the modern type, this "new
woman" business, would repel him; and here she
was, making him positively look forward to the
glimpse of her safety bicycle careering along the

lakeside road. And she, too, had never met anyone like *him*. She had always thought that
middle-aged men who read the *Times* and disap-
proved of modernity were terrible bores; yet here
he was, claiming her interest and attention far
more than youths of her own age. She liked
him, initially, because he was so hard to get to
know, because he had gentle and quiet manners,
because his opinions dated from those utterly im-
possible seventies and eighties and even earlier —
yet were, for all that, so thoroughly honest; and
because — because his eyes were brown and he
looked charming when he smiled. "Of course, *I*
shall call you Chips, too," she said, when she
learned that was his nickname at school.

Within a week they were head over heels in
love; before Chips could walk without a stick,
they considered themselves engaged; and they
were married in London a week before the beginning of the autumn term.

When Chips, dreaming through the hours at Mrs. Wickett's, recollected those days, he used to look down at his feet and wonder which one it was that had performed so signal a service. That, the trivial cause of so many momentous happenings, was the one thing of which details evaded him. But he resaw the glorious hump of the Gable (he had never visited the Lake District since), and the mouse-gray depths of Wastwater under the Screes; he could resmell the washed air after heavy rain, and refollow the ribbon of the pass across to Sty Head. So clearly it lingered, that time of dizzy happiness, those evening strolls by the waterside, her cool voice and her gay laughter. She had been a very happy person, always.

They had both been so eager, planning a future together; but he had been rather serious about it, even a little awed. It would be all right, of course, her coming to Brookfield; other housemasters were married. And she liked boys, she told him, and would enjoy living among them. "Oh, Chips, I'm so glad you are what you are. I was afraid you were a solicitor or a stockbroker or a dentist or a man with a big cotton business in Manchester. When I first met you, I mean. Schoolmastering's so different, so important, don't you think? To be influencing those who are going to grow up and matter to the world . . ."

Chips said he hadn't thought of it like that

—or, at least, not often. He did his best; that was all anyone could do in any job.

"Yes, of course, Chips. I do love you for saying simple things like that."

And one morning — another memory gem-clear when he turned to it — he had for some reason been afflicted with an acute desire to depreciate himself and all his attainments. He had told her of his only mediocre degree, of his occasional difficulties of discipline, of the certainty that he would never get a promotion, and of his complete ineligibility to marry a young and ambitious girl. And at the end of it all she had laughed in answer.

She had no parents and was married from the house of an aunt in Ealing. On the night before the wedding, when Chips left the house to return to his hotel, she said, with mock gravity: "This is an occasion, you know — this last farewell of ours. I feel rather like a new boy beginning

33

his first term with you. Not scared, mind you
— but just, for once, in a thoroughly respectful
mood. Shall I call you 'sir' — or would 'Mr.
Chips' be the right thing? 'Mr. Chips,' I think.
Good-bye, then — good-bye, Mr. Chips. . . ."

(A hansom clop-clopping in the roadway;
green-pale gas lamps flickering on a wet pave-
ment; newsboys shouting something about South
Africa; Sherlock Holmes in Baker Street.)

"Good-bye, Mr. Chips . . ."

THERE had followed then a time of such happiness that Chips, remembering it long afterward, hardly believed it could ever have happened before or since in the world. For his marriage was a triumphant success. Katherine conquered Brookfield as she had conquered Chips; she was immensely popular with boys and masters alike. Even the wives of the masters, tempted at first to be jealous of one so young and lovely, could not long resist her charms.

35

But most remarkable of all was the change she made in Chips. Till his marriage he had been a dry and rather neutral sort of person; liked and thought well of by Brookfield in general, but not of the stuff that makes for great popularity or that stirs great affection. He had been at Brookfield for over a quarter of a century, long enough to have established himself as a decent fellow and a hard worker; but just too long for anyone to believe him capable of ever being much more. He had, in fact, already begun to sink into that creeping dry rot of pedagogy which is the worst and ultimate pitfall of the profession; giving the same lessons year after year had formed a groove into which the other affairs of his life adjusted themselves with insidious ease. He worked well; he was conscientious; he was a fixture that gave service, satisfaction, confidence, everything except inspiration.

36

And then came this astonishing girl-wife whom
nobody had expected — least of all Chips himself.
She made him, to all appearances, a new man;
though most of the newness was really a warm-
ing to life of things that were old, imprisoned,
and unguessed. His eyes gained sparkle; his
mind, which was adequately if not brilliantly
equipped, began to move more adventurously.
The one thing he had always had, a sense of
humor, blossomed into a sudden richness to
which his years lent maturity. He began to
feel a greater sureness; his discipline improved
to a point at which it could become, in a sense,
less rigid; he became more popular. When he
had first come to Brookfield he had aimed to be
loved, honored, and obeyed — but obeyed, at any
rate. Obedience he had secured, and honor had
been granted him; but only now came love,
the sudden love of boys for a man who was
kind without being soft, who understood them

37

well enough, but not too much, and whose private happiness linked them with their own. He began to make little jokes, the sort that schoolboys like — mnemonics and puns that raised laughs and at the same time imprinted something in the mind. There was one that never failed to please, though it was only a sample of many others. Whenever his Roman History forms came to deal with the Lex Canuleia, the law that permitted patricians to marry plebeians, Chips used to add: "So that, you see, if Miss Plebs wanted Mr. Patrician to marry her, and he said he couldn't, she probably replied: 'Oh yes, you can, you liar!'" Roars of laughter.

And Kathie broadened his views and opinions, also, giving him an outlook far beyond the roofs and turrets of Brookfield, so that he saw his country as something deep and gracious to which Brookfield was but one of many feeding streams. She had a cleverer brain than his, and he could

38

not confute her ideas even if and when he disagreed with them; he remained, for instance, a Conservative in politics, despite all her radical-socialist talk. But even where he did not accept, he absorbed; her young idealism worked upon his maturity to produce an amalgam very gentle and wise.

Sometimes she persuaded him completely. Brookfield, for example, ran a mission in East London, to which boys and parents contributed generously with money but rarely with personal contact. It was Katherine who suggested that a team from the mission should come up to Brookfield and play one of the School's elevens at soccer. The idea was so revolutionary that from anyone but Katherine it could not have survived its first frosty reception. To introduce a group of slum boys to the serene pleasaunces of better-class youngsters seemed at first a wanton stirring of all kinds of things that had better be left untouched. The whole staff was against it, and the School, if its opinion could have been taken, was probably against it too. Everyone was certain that the East End lads would be hooligans, or else that they would be made to feel uncomfortable; anyhow, there would be "incidents," and everyone would be confused and upset. Yet Katherine persisted.

"Chips," she said, "they're wrong, you know, and I'm right. I'm looking ahead to the future, they and you are looking back to the past. England isn't always going to be divided into officers and 'other ranks.' And those Poplar boys are just as important — to England — as Brookfield is. You've got to have them here, Chips. You can't satisfy your conscience by writing a check for a few guineas and keeping them at arm's length. Besides, they're proud of Brookfield — just as you are. Years hence, maybe, boys of that sort will be coming here — a few of them, at any

rate. Why not? Why ever not? Chips, dear,
remember this is eighteen-ninety-seven — not
sixty-seven, when you were up at Cambridge.
You got your ideas well stuck in those days,
and good ideas they were too, a lot of them.
But a few — just a few, Chips — want unstick-
ing. . . ."

Rather to her surprise, he gave way and
suddenly became a keen advocate of the proposal,
and the *volte-face* was so complete that the au-
thorities were taken unawares and found themselves consenting to the dangerous experiment.
The boys from Poplar arrived at Brookfield one
Saturday afternoon, played soccer with the
School's second team, were honorably defeated
by seven goals to five, and later had high tea
with the School team in the Dining Hall. They
then met the Head and were shown over the
School, and Chips saw them off at the railway
station in the evening. Everything had passed

without the slightest hitch of any kind, and it was clear that the visitors were taking away with them as fine an impression as they had left behind.

They took back with them also the memory of a charming woman who had met them and talked to them; for once, years later, during the War, a private stationed at a big military camp near Brookfield called on Chips and said he had been one of that first visiting team. Chips gave him tea and chatted with him, till at length, shaking hands, the man said: "And 'ow's the missus, sir? I remember her very well."

"Do you?" Chips answered, eagerly. "Do you remember her?"

"Rather. I should think anyone would."

And Chips replied: "They don't, you know. At least, not here. Boys come and go; new faces all the time; memories don't last. Even masters don't stay forever. Since last year—when old

Gribble retired — he's — um — the School butler — there hasn't been anyone here who ever saw my wife. She died, you know, less than a year after your visit. In ninety-eight."

"I'm real sorry to 'ear that, sir. There's two or three o' my pals, anyhow, who remember 'er clear as anything, though we did only see 'er that wunst. Yes, we remember 'er, all right."

"I'm very glad. . . . That was a grand day we all had — and a fine game, too."

"One o' the best days aht I ever 'ad in me life. Wish it was then and not nah — straight, I do. I'm off to Frawnce to-morrer."

A month or so later Chips heard that he had been killed at Passchendaele.

And so it stood, a warm and vivid patch in his
life, casting a radiance that glowed in a thousand
recollections. Twilight at Mrs. Wickett's, when
the School bell clanged for call-over, brought
them back to him in a cloud — Katherine scam-
pering along the stone corridors, laughing beside
him at some "howler" in an essay he was mark-
ing, taking the cello part in a Mozart trio for
the School concert, her creamy arm sweeping
over the brown sheen of the instrument. She

had been a good player and a fine musician.
And Katherine furred and muffed for the December
house matches, Katherine at the Garden
Party that followed Speech Day Prize-giving,
Katherine tendering her advice in any little problem
that arose. Good advice, too—which he
did not always take, but which always influenced
him.

"Chips, dear, I'd let them off if I were you.
After all, it's nothing very serious."

"I know. I'd like to let them off, but if I
do I'm afraid they'll do it again."

"Try telling them that, frankly, and give
them the chance."

"I might."

And there were other things, occasionally,
that *were* serious.

"You know, Chips, having all these hundreds
of boys cooped up here is really an unnatural
arrangement, when you come to think about it.

So that when anything does occur that ought n't to, don't you think it 's a bit unfair to come down on them as if it were their own fault for being here?"

"Don't know about that, Kathie, but I do know that for everybody's sake we have to be pretty strict about this sort of thing. One black sheep can contaminate others."

"After he himself has been contaminated to begin with. After all, that 's what probably *did* happen, is n't it?"

"Maybe. We can't help it. Anyhow, I believe Brookfield is better than a lot of other schools. All the more reason to keep it so."

"But this boy, Chips . . . you 're going to sack him?"

"The Head probably will, when I tell him."

"And you 're going to tell the Head?"

"It 's a duty, I 'm afraid."

"Could n't you think about it a bit . . . talk

46

"Couldn't you think
about it a bit ..."

to the boy again . . . find out how it began . . .
After all — apart from this business — is n't he
rather a nice boy?"

"Oh, he 's all right."

"Then, Chips dear, don't you think there
ought to be some other way . . ."

And so on. About once in ten times he was
adamant and would n't be persuaded.¯ In about
half of these exceptional cases he afterward
rather wished he had taken her advice. And
years later, whenever he had trouble with a boy,
he was always at the mercy of a softening wave
of reminiscence; the boy would stand there, waiting to be told his punishment, and would see, if
he were observant, the brown eyes twinkle into
a shine that told him all was well. But he did
not guess that at such a moment Chips was re-
membering something that had happened long
before he was born; that Chips was thinking:
Young ruffian, I 'm hanged if *I* can think of any

reason to let him off, but I 'll bet *she* would have done!

But she had not always pleaded for leniency. On rather rare occasions she urged severity where Chips was inclined to be forgiving. "I don't like his type, Chips. He's too cocksure of himself. If he's looking for trouble I should certainly let him have it."

What a host of little incidents, all deep-buried in the past — problems that had once been urgent, arguments that had once been keen, anecdotes that were funny only because one remembered the fun. Did any emotion really matter when the last trace of it had vanished from human memory; and if that were so, what a crowd of emotions clung to him as to their last home before annihilation! He must be kind to them, must treasure them in his mind before their long sleep. That affair of Archer's resignation, for instance — a queer business, that was.

And that affair about the rat that Dunster put
in the organ loft while old Ogilvie was taking
choir practice. Ogilvie was dead and Dunster
drowned at Jutland; of others who had witnessed
or heard of the incident, probably most had forgotten. And it had been like that, with other
incidents, for centuries. He had a sudden vision
of thousands and thousands of boys, from the age
of Elizabeth onward; dynasty upon dynasty of
masters; long epochs of Brookfield history that
had left not even a ghostly record. Who knew
why the old fifth-form room was called "the
Pit"? There was probably a reason, to begin
with; but it had since been lost — lost like the
lost books of Livy. And what happened at
Brookfield when Cromwell fought at Naseby,
near by? How did Brookfield react to the great
scare of the "Forty-Five"? Was there a whole
holiday when news came of Waterloo? And so
on, up to the earliest time that he himself could

remember — 1870, and Wetherby saying, by way of small talk after their first and only interview: "Looks as if we shall have to settle with the Prussians ourselves one of these fine days, eh?"

When Chips remembered things like this he often felt that he would write them down and make a book of them; and during his years at Mrs. Wickett's he sometimes went even so far as to make desultory notes in an exercise book. But he was soon brought up against difficulties — the chief one being that writing tired him, both mentally and physically. Somehow, too, his recollections lost much of their flavor when they were written down; that story about Rushton and the sack of potatoes, for instance — it would seem quite tame in print, but Lord, how funny it had been at the time! It was funny, too, to remember it; though perhaps if you did n't remember Rushton . . . and who would, anyway, after all those years? It was such a long time ago . . . Mrs. Wickett, did you ever know a fellow named Rushton? Before your time, I dare say . . . went to Burma in some government job . . . or was it Borneo? . . . Very funny fellow, Rushton. . . .

And there he was, dreaming again before the fire, dreaming of times and incidents in which he alone could take secret interest. Funny and sad, comic and tragic, they all mixed up in his mind, and some day, however hard it proved, he *would* sort them out and make a book of them. . . .

VIII

AND there was always in his mind that spring
day in ninety-eight when he had paced through
Brookfield village as in some horrifying night-
mare, half struggling to escape into an outside
world where the sun still shone and where everything had happened differently. Young Faulk-
ner had met him there in the lane outside the
School. "Please, sir, may I have the afternoon
off? My people are coming up."

"Eh? What's that? Oh yes, yes. . . ."

"Can I miss Chapel, too, sir?"

"Yes . . . yes . . ."

"And may I go to the station to meet them?"

He nearly answered: "You can go to blazes for all I care. My wife is dead and my child is dead, and I wish I were dead myself."

Actually he nodded and stumbled on. He did not want to talk to anybody or to receive condolences; he wanted to get used to things, if he could, before facing the kind words of others. He took his fourth form as usual after call-over, setting them grammar to learn by heart while he himself stayed at his desk in a cold, continuing trance. Suddenly someone said: "Please, sir, there are a lot of letters for you."

So there were; he had been leaning his elbows on them; they were all addressed to him by name. He tore them open one after the other, but each contained nothing but a blank sheet of paper. He thought in a distant way that it was

55

rather peculiar, but he made no comment; the incident gave hardly an impact upon his vastly greater preoccupations. Not till days afterward did he realize that it had been a piece of April foolery.

They had died on the same day, the mother and the child just born; on April 1, 1898.

IX

CHIPS changed his more commodious apartments in School House for his old original bachelor quarters. He thought at first he would give up his housemastership, but the Head persuaded him otherwise; and later he was glad. The work gave him something to do, filled up an emptiness in his mind and heart. He was different; everyone noticed it. Just as marriage had added something, so did bereavement; after the first stupor of grief he became suddenly the kind of man whom boys, at any rate, unhesitatingly classed as "old." It was not that he was less active; he could still knock up a half century on the cricket field; nor was it that he had lost any interest or keenness in his work. Actually, too, his hair had been graying for years; yet now, for the first time, people seemed to notice it. He was fifty. Once, after some energetic fives, during which he had played as well as many a fellow half his age, he overheard a boy saying: "Not half bad for an old chap like him."

Chips, when he was over eighty, used to recount that incident with many chuckles. "Old at fifty, eh? Umph — it was Naylor who said that, and Naylor can't be far short of fifty himself by now! I wonder if he still thinks that fifty's such an age? Last I heard of him, he was lawyering, and lawyers live long — look at Halsbury — umph — Chancellor at eighty-two, and died at ninety-nine. There's an — umph — age for you! Too old at fifty — why, fellows like that are too *young* at fifty. . . . I was myself . . . a mere infant. . . ."

And there was a sense in which it was true. For with the new century there settled upon Chips a mellowness that gathered all his developing mannerisms and his oft-repeated jokes into a single harmony. No longer did he have those slight and occasional disciplinary troubles, or feel diffident about his own work and worth. He found that his pride in Brookfield reflected back, giving him cause for pride in himself and his position. It was a service that gave him freedom to be supremely and completely himself. He had won, by seniority and ripeness, an uncharted no-man's-land of privilege; he had acquired the right to those gentle eccentricities that so often attack schoolmasters and parsons. He wore his gown till it was almost too tattered to hold together; and when he stood on the wooden bench by Big Hall steps to take call-over, it was with an air of mystic abandonment to ritual. He held the School List, a long sheet curling over a board; and each boy, as he passed, spoke his own name for Chips to verify and then tick off on the list. That verifying glance was an easy and favorite subject of mimicry throughout the School — steel-rimmed spectacles slipping down the nose, eyebrows lifted, one a little higher than the other, a gaze half rapt, half quizzical. And on windy days, with gown and white hair and School List fluttering in uproarious confusion, the whole thing became a comic turn sandwiched between afternoon games and the return to classes.

Some of those names, in little snatches of a chorus, recurred to him ever afterward without any effort of memory. . . . Ainsworth, Attwood, Avonmore, Babcock, Baggs, Barnard, Bassen-

When he stood....
to take call-over

thwaite, Battersby, Beccles, Bedford-Marshall, Bentley, Best . . .

Another one: —

. . . Unsley, Vailes, Wadham, Wagstaff, Wallington, Waters Primus, Waters Secundus, Watling, Waveney, Webb . . .

And yet another that comprised, as he used to tell his fourth-form Latinists, an excellent example of a hexameter: —

. . . Lancaster, Latton, Lemare, Lytton-Bosworth, MacGonigall, Mansfield . . .

Where had they all gone to, he often pondered; those threads he had once held together, how far had they scattered, some to break, others to weave into unknown patterns? The strange randomness of the world beguiled him, that randomness which never would, so long as the world lasted, give meaning to those choruses again.

And behind Brookfield, as one may glimpse

a mountain behind another mountain when the mist clears, he saw the world of change and conflict; and he saw it, more than he realized, with the remembered eyes of Kathie. She had not been able to bequeath him all her mind, still less the brilliance of it; but she had left him with a calmness and a poise that accorded well with his own inward emotions. It was typical of him that he did not share the general jingo bitterness against the Boers. Not that he was a pro-Boer — he was far too traditional for that, and he disliked the kind of people who *were* pro-Boers; but still, it did cross his mind at times that the Boers were engaged in a struggle that had a curious similarity to those of certain English history-book heroes — Hereward the Wake, for instance, or Caractacus. He once tried to shock his fifth form by suggesting this, but they only thought it was one of his little jokes.

However heretical he might be about the

Boers, he was orthodox about Mr. Lloyd George and the famous Budget. He did not care for either of them. And when, years later, L. G. came as the guest of honor to a Brookfield Speech Day, Chips said, on being presented to him: "Mr. Lloyd George, I am nearly old enough — umph — to remember you as a young man, and — umph — I confess that you seem to me — umph — to have improved — umph — a great deal." The Head, standing with them, was rather aghast; but L. G. laughed heartily and talked to Chips more than to anyone else during the ceremonial that followed.

"Just like Chips," was commented afterward. "He gets away with it. I suppose at that age anything you say to anybody is all right. . . ."

X

In 1900 old Meldrum, who had succeeded
Wetherby as Head and had held office for three
decades, died suddenly from pneumonia; and
in the interval before the appointment of a successor, Chips became Acting Head of Brookfield.
There was just the faintest chance that the Governors might make the appointment a permanent
one; but Chips was not really disappointed when
they brought in a youngster of thirty-seven, glit-
tering with Firsts and Blues and with the kind

of personality that could reduce Big Hall to silence by the mere lifting of an eyebrow. Chips was not in the running with that kind of person; he never had been and never would be, and he knew it. He was an altogether milder and less ferocious animal.

Those years before his retirement in 1913 were studded with sharply remembered pictures.

A May morning; the clang of the School bell at an unaccustomed time; everyone summoned to assemble in Big Hall. Ralston, the new Head, very pontifical and aware of himself, fixing the multitude with a cold, presaging severity. "You will all be deeply grieved to hear that His Majesty King Edward the Seventh died this morning. . . . There will be no school this afternoon, but a service will be held in the Chapel at **four-thirty**."

A summer morning on the railway line near Brookfield. The railwaymen were on strike, soldiers were driving the engines, stones had been thrown at trains. Brookfield boys were patrolling the line, thinking the whole business great fun. Chips, who was in charge, stood a little way off, talking to a man at the gate of a cottage. Young Cricklade approached. "Please, sir, what shall we do if we meet any strikers?"

"Would you like to meet one?"

"I — I don't know, sir."

God bless the boy — he talked of them as if they were queer animals out of a zoo! "Well, here you are, then — umph — you can meet Mr. Jones — he's a striker. When he's on duty he has charge of the signal box at the station. You've put your life in his hands many a time."

Afterward the story went round the School: There was Chips, talking to a striker. Talking to a striker. Might have been quite friendly, the way they were talking together.

68

Chips, thinking it over a good many times, always added to himself that Kathie would have approved, and would also have been amused.

Because always, whatever happened and however the avenues of politics twisted and curved, he had faith in England, in English flesh and blood, and in Brookfield as a place whose ultimate worth depended on whether she fitted herself into the English scene with dignity and without disproportion. He had been left a vision that grew clearer with each year — of an England for which days of ease were nearly over, of a nation steering into channels where a hair's breadth of error might be catastrophic. He remembered the Diamond Jubilee; there had been a whole holiday at Brookfield, and he had taken Kathie to London to see the procession. That old and legendary lady, sitting in her carriage like some crumbling wooden doll, had symbolized impressively so many things that, like herself, were nearing an end. Was it only the century, or was it an epoch?

And then that frenzied Edwardian decade, like an electric lamp that goes brighter and whiter just before it burns itself out.

Strikes and lockouts, champagne suppers and unemployed marchers, Chinese labor, tariff reform, *H.M.S. Dreadnought,* Marconi, Home Rule for Ireland, Doctor Crippen, suffragettes, the lines of Chatalja. . . .

An April evening, windy and rainy; the fourth form construing Vergil, not very intelligently, for there was exciting news in the papers; young Grayson, in particular, was careless and preoccupied. A quiet, nervous boy.

"Grayson, stay behind — umph — after the rest."

Then: —

"Grayson, I don't want to be — umph — severe, because you are generally pretty good — umph

— in your work, but to-day — you don't seem — umph — to have been trying at all. Is anything the matter?"

"N-no, sir."

"Well — umph — we'll say no more about it, but — umph — I shall expect better things next time."

Next morning it was noised around the School that Grayson's father had sailed on the *Titanic,* and that no news had yet come through as to his fate.

Grayson was excused lessons; for a whole day the School centred emotionally upon his anxieties. Then came news that his father had been among those rescued.

Chips shook hands with the boy. "Well, umph — I'm delighted, Grayson. A happy ending. You must be feeling pretty pleased with life."

"Y-yes, sir."

A quiet, nervous boy. And it was Grayson Senior, not Junior, with whom Chips was destined later to condole.

And then the row with Ralston. Funny thing,
Chips had never liked him; he was efficient,
ruthless, ambitious, but not, somehow, very lik-
able. He had, admittedly, raised the status of
Brookfield as a school, and for the first time
in memory there was a longish waiting list.
Ralston was a live wire; a fine power transmitter,
but you had to beware of him.

Chips had never bothered to beware of him;
he was not attracted by the man, but he served

73

him willingly enough and quite loyally. Or, rather, he served Brookfield. He knew that Ralston did not like him, either; but that did n't seem to matter. He felt himself sufficiently protected by age and seniority from the fate of other masters whom Ralston had failed to like.

Then suddenly, in 1908, when he had just turned sixty, came Ralston's urbane ultimatum. "Mr. Chipping, have you ever thought you would like to retire?"

Chips stared about him in that book-lined study, startled by the question, wondering why Ralston should have asked it. He said, at length: "No — umph — I can't say that — umph — I have thought much about it — umph — yet."

"Well, Mr. Chipping, the suggestion is there for you to consider. The Governors would, of course, agree to your being adequately pensioned."

Abruptly Chips flamed up. "But — umph —

I don't want — to retire. I don't — umph — need to consider it."

"Nevertheless, I suggest that you do."

"But — umph — I don't see — why — I should!"

"In that case, things are going to be a little difficult."

"Difficult? Why — difficult?"

And then they set to, Ralston getting cooler and harder, Chips getting warmer and more passionate, till at last Ralston said, icily: "Since you force me to use plain words, Mr. Chipping, you shall have them. For some time past, you haven't been pulling your weight here. Your methods of teaching are slack and old-fashioned; your personal habits are slovenly; and you ignore my instructions in a way which, in a younger man, I should regard as rank insubordination. It won't do, Mr. Chipping, and you must ascribe it to my forbearance that I have put up with it so long."

75

"But — " Chips began, in sheer bewilderment; and then he took up isolated words out of that extraordinary indictment. *"Slovenly* — umph — you said — ?"

"Yes, look at the gown you're wearing. I happen to know that that gown of yours is a subject of continual amusement throughout the School."

Chips knew it, too, but it had never seemed to him a very regrettable matter.

He went on: "And — you also said — umph — something about — *insubordination* — ?"

"No, I didn't. I said that in a younger man I should have regarded it as that. In your case it's probably a mixture of slackness and obstinacy. This question of Latin pronunciation, for instance — I think I told you years ago that I wanted the new style used throughout the School. The other masters obeyed me; you prefer to stick to your old methods, and the result is simply chaos and inefficiency."

76

At last Chips had something tangible that he could tackle. "Oh, *that!*" he answered scornfully. "Well, I — umph — I admit that I don't agree with the new pronunciation. I never did. Umph — a lot of nonsense, in my opinion. Making boys say 'Kickero' at school when — umph — for the rest of their lives they'll say 'Cicero' — if they ever — umph — say it at all. And instead of 'vicissim' — God bless my soul — you'd make them say, 'We kiss 'im'! Umph — umph!" And he chuckled momentarily, forgetting that he was in Ralston's study and not in his own friendly form room.

"Well, there you are, Mr. Chipping — that's just an example of what I complain of. You hold one opinion and I hold another, and, since you decline to give way, there can't very well be any alternative. I aim to make Brookfield a thoroughly up-to-date school. I'm a science man myself, but for all that I have no objection to

77

the classics — provided that they are taught effi-
ciently. Because they are dead languages is no
reason why they should be dealt with in a dead
educational technique. I understand, Mr. Chipping, that your Latin and Greek lessons are
exactly the same as they were when I began
here ten years ago?"

Chips answered, slowly and with pride: "For
that matter — umph — they are the same as when
your predecessor — Mr. Meldrum — came here,
and that — umph — was thirty-eight years ago.
We began here, Mr. Meldrum and I — in —
umph — in 1870. And it was — um — Mr. Meldrum's predecessor, Mr. Wetherby — who first
approved my syllabus. 'You'll take the Cicero
for the fourth,' he said to me. Cicero, too — not
Kickero!"

"Very interesting, Mr. Chipping, but once
again it proves my point — you live too much in
the past, and not enough in the present and

future. Times are changing, whether you realize it or not. Modern parents are beginning to demand something more for their three years' school fees than a few scraps of languages that nobody speaks. Besides, your boys don't learn even what they're supposed to learn. None of them last year got through the Lower Certificate."

And suddenly, in a torrent of thoughts too pressing to be put into words, Chips made answer to himself. These examinations and certificates and so on — what did they matter? And all this efficiency and up-to-dateness — what did *that* matter, either? Ralston was trying to run Brookfield like a factory — a factory for turning out a snob culture based on money and machines. The old gentlemanly traditions of family and broad acres were changing, as doubtless they were bound to; but instead of widening them to form a genuine inclusive democracy of duke

79

and dustman, Ralston was narrowing them upon the single issue of a fat banking account. There never had been so many rich men's sons at Brookfield. The Speech Day Garden Party was like Ascot. Ralston met these wealthy fellows in London clubs and persuaded them that Brookfield was *the* coming school, and, since they could n't buy their way into Eton or Harrow, they greedily swallowed the bait. Awful fellows, some of them — though others were decent enough. Financiers, company promoters, pill manufacturers. One of them gave his son five pounds a week pocket money. Vulgar . . . ostentatious . . . all the hectic rotten-ripeness of the age. . . . And once Chips had got into trouble because of some joke he had made about a boy's name. The boy wrote home about it, and his father sent an angry letter to Ralston. Touchy, no sense of humor, no sense of proportion — that

was the matter with them, these new fellows.
. . . No sense of proportion. And it was a sense
of proportion, above all things, that Brookfield
ought to teach — not so much Latin or Greek
or Chemistry or Mechanics. And you couldn't
expect to test that sense of proportion by setting
papers and granting certificates. . . .

All this flashed through his mind in an instant
of protest and indignation, but he did not say
a word of it. He merely gathered his tattered
gown together and with an "umph — umph"
walked a few paces away. He had had enough
of the argument. At the door he turned and
said: "I don't — umph — intend to resign — and
you can — umph — do what you like about it!"

Looking back upon that scene in the calm
perspective of a quarter of a century, Chips could
find it in his heart to feel a little sorry for
Ralston. Particularly when, as it happened, Ralston had been in such complete ignorance of

the forces he was dealing with. So, for that matter, had Chips himself. Neither had correctly estimated the toughness of Brookfield tradition, and its readiness to defend itself and its defenders. For it had so chanced that a small boy, waiting to see Ralston that morning, had been listening outside the door during the whole of the interview; he had been thrilled by it, naturally, and had told his friends. Some of these, in a surprisingly short time, had told their parents; so that very soon it was common knowledge that Ralston had insulted Chips and had demanded his resignation. The amazing result was a spontaneous outburst of sympathy and partisanship such as Chips, in his wildest dreams, had never envisaged. He found, rather to his astonishment, that Ralston was thoroughly unpopular; he was feared and respected, but not liked; and in this issue of Chips the dislike rose to a point where it conquered fear and demolished even respect. There was talk of having some kind of public riot in the School if Ralston succeeded in banishing Chips. The masters, many of them young men who agreed that Chips was hopelessly old-fashioned, rallied round him nevertheless because they hated Ralston's slave driving and saw in the old veteran a likely champion. And one day the Chairman of the Governors, Sir John Rivers, visited Brookfield, ignored Ralston, and went direct to Chips. "A fine fellow, Rivers," Chips would say, telling the story to Mrs. Wickett for the dozenth time. "Not — umph — a very brilliant boy in class. I remember he could never — umph — master his verbs. And now — umph — I see in the papers — they've made him — umph — a baronet. It just shows you — umph — it just shows you."

Sir John had said, on that morning in 1908, taking Chips by the arm as they walked round the deserted cricket pitches: "Chips, old boy, I hear you've been having the deuce of a row with Ralston. Sorry to hear about it, for your sake — but I want you to know that the Governors are with you to a man. We don't like the fellow a great deal. Very clever and all that, but a bit too clever, if you ask me. Claims to have doubled the School's endowment funds by some monkeying on the Stock Exchange. Dare say he has, but a chap like that wants watching. So if he starts chucking his weight about with you, tell him very politely he can go to the devil. The Governors don't want you to resign. Brookfield wouldn't be the same without you, and they know it. We all know it. You can stay here till you're a hundred if you feel like it — indeed, it's our hope that you will."

And at that — both then and often when he recounted it afterward — Chips broke down.

XII

So he stayed on at Brookfield, having as little to do with Ralston as possible. And in 1911 Ralston left, "to better himself"; he was offered the headship of one of the greater public schools. His successor was a man named Chatteris, whom Chips liked; he was even younger than Ralston had been — thirty-four. He was supposed to be very brilliant; at any rate, he was modern (Natural Sciences Tripos), friendly, and sympathetic. Recognizing in Chips a Brookfield in-

85

stitution, he courteously and wisely accepted the situation.

In 1913 Chips had had bronchitis and was off duty for nearly the whole of the winter term. It was that which made him decide to resign that summer, when he was sixty-five. After all, it was a good, ripe age; and Ralston's straight words had, in some ways, had an effect. He felt that it would not be fair to hang on if he could not decently do his job. Besides, he would not sever himself completely. He would take rooms across the road, with the excellent Mrs. Wickett who had once been linen-room maid; he could visit the School whenever he wanted, and could still, in a sense, remain a part of it.

At that final end-of-term dinner, in July 1913, Chips received his farewell presentations and made a speech. It was not a very long speech, but it had a good many jokes in it, and was made twice as long, perhaps, by the laughter that im

86

peded its progress. There were several Latin quotations in it, as well as a reference to the Captain of the School, who, Chips said, had been guilty of exaggeration in speaking of his (Chips's) services to Brookfield. "But then — umph — he comes of an — umph — exaggerating family. I — um — remember — once — having to thrash his father — for it. [Laughter] I gave him one mark — umph — for a Latin translation, and he — umph — exaggerated the one into a seven! Umph — umph!" Roars of laughter and tumultuous cheers! A typical Chips remark, everyone thought.

And then he mentioned that he had been at Brookfield for forty-two years, and that he had been very happy there. "It has been my life," he said, simply. *"O mihi praeteritos referat si Jupiter annos. . . .* Umph — I need not — of course — translate. . . ." Much laughter. "I remember lots of changes at Brookfield. I remember the — um — the first bicycle. I remember when there was no gas or electric light and we used to have a member of the domestic staff called a lamp-boy — he did nothing else but clean and trim and light lamps throughout the School. I remember when there was a hard frost that lasted for seven weeks in the winter term — there were no games, and the whole School learned to skate on the fens. Eighteen-eighty-something, that was. I remember when two thirds of the School went down with German measles and Big Hall was turned into a hospital ward. I remember the great bonfire we had on Mafeking night. It was lit too near the pavilion and we had to send for the fire brigade to put it out. And the firemen were having their own celebrations and most of them were — um — in a regrettable condition. [Laughter] I remember Mrs. Brool, whose photograph is still in the tuckshop; she served there until an uncle in Australia left her a lot of money. In fact, I remember so much that I often think I ought to write a book. Now what should I call it? 'Memories of Rod and Lines' — eh? [Cheers and laughter. That was a good one, people thought — one of Chips's best.] Well, well, perhaps I shall write it, some day. But I'd rather tell you about it, really. I remember . . . I remember . . . but chiefly I remember all your faces. I never forget them. I have thousands of faces in my mind — the faces of boys. If you come and see me again in years to come — as I hope you all will — I shall try to remember those older faces of yours, but it's just possible I shan't be able to — and then some day you'll see me somewhere and I shan't recognize you and you'll say to yourself, 'The old boy doesn't remember me.' [Laughter] But I *do* remember you — as you are *now*. That's the point. In my mind you never grow up at all. Never. Sometimes, for instance, when people talk to me about our respected Chairman of the Governors, I think to myself, 'Ah yes, a jolly little chap with hair that sticks up on top — and absolutely no idea whatever about the difference between a Gerund and a Gerundive.' [Loud laughter] Well, well, I must n't go on — umph — all night. Think of me sometimes as I shall certainly think of you. *Haec olim meminisse juvabit* . . . again I need not translate." Much laughter and shouting and prolonged cheers.

August 1913. Chips went for a cure to Wiesbaden, where he lodged at the home of the German master at Brookfield, Herr Staefel, with whom he had become friendly. Staefel was thirty years his junior, but the two men got on excellently. In September, when term began, Chips returned and took up residence at Mrs. Wickett's. He felt a great deal stronger and fitter after his holiday, and almost wished he had not retired. Nevertheless, he found plenty to do. He had all the new boys to tea. He watched all the important matches on the Brookfield ground. Once a term he dined with the Head, and once also with the masters. He took on the preparation and editing of a new Brookfeldian Directory. He accepted presidency of the Old Boys' Club and went to dinners in London. He wrote occasional articles, full of jokes and Latin quotations, for the Brookfield terminal magazine. He read his *Times* every morning — very thoroughly; and he also began to read detective stories — he had been keen on them ever since the first thrills of Sherlock. Yes, he was quite busy, and quite happy, too.

A year later, in 1914, he again attended the end-of-term dinner. There was a lot of war talk — civil war in Ulster, and trouble between Austria and Serbia. Herr Staefel, who was leaving for Germany the next day, told Chips he thought the Balkan business would n't come to anything.

THE War years.

The first shock, and then the first optimism. The Battle of the Marne, the Russian steam-roller, Kitchener.

"Do you think it will last long, sir?"

Chips, questioned as he watched the first trial game of the season, gave quite a cheery answer. He was, like thousands of others, hopelessly wrong; but, unlike thousands of others, he did not afterward conceal the fact. "We ought to have — um — finished it — um — by Christmas. The Germans are already beaten. But why? Are you thinking of — um — joining up, Forrester?"

Joke — because Forrester was the smallest new boy Brookfield had ever had — about four feet high above his muddy football boots. (But not so much a joke, when you came to think of it afterward; for he was killed in 1918 — shot down in flames over Cambrai.) But one didn't guess what lay ahead. It seemed tragically sensational when the first Old Brookfeldian was killed in action — in September. Chips thought, when that news came: A hundred years ago boys from the school were fighting *against* the French. Strange, in a way, that the sacrifices of one generation should so cancel out those of another. He tried to express this to Blades, the Head of School House; but Blades, eighteen years old and already in training for a cadetship, only laughed. What

93

had all that history stuff to do with it, anyhow?
Just old Chips with one of his queer ideas, that's
all.

1915. Armies clenched in deadlock from the
sea to Switzerland. The Dardanelles. Gallip-
oli. Military camps springing up quite near
Brookfield; soldiers using the playing fields
for sports and training; swift developments of
Brookfield O.T.C. Most of the younger masters gone or in uniform. Every Sunday night,
in the Chapel after evening service, Chatteris
read out the names of old boys killed, together
with short biographies. Very moving; but
Chips, in the back pew under the gallery,
thought: They are only names to him; he does n't
see their faces as I do. . . .

1916. . . . The Somme Battle. Twenty-three
names read out one Sunday evening.

Toward the close of that catastrophic July,
Chatteris talked to Chips one afternoon at Mrs.

Wickett's. He was overworked and overworried
and looked very ill. "To tell you the truth,
Chipping, I'm not having too easy a time here.
I'm thirty-nine, you know, and unmarried, and
lots of people seem to think they know what I
ought to do. Also, I happen to be diabetic, and
could n't pass the blindest M.O., but I don't see
why I should pin a medical certificate on my
front door."

Chips had n't known anything about this; it
was a shock to him, for he liked Chatteris.

The latter continued: "You see how it is. Ralston filled the place up with young men — all
very good, of course — but now most of them have
joined up and the substitutes are pretty dreadful,
on the whole. They poured ink down a man's
neck in prep one night last week — silly fool —
got hysterical. I have to take classes myself, take
prep for fools like that, work till midnight every
night, and get cold-shouldered as a slacker on top

95

of everything. I can't stand it much longer. If things don't improve next term I shall have a breakdown."

"I do sympathize with you," Chips said.

"I hoped you would. And that brings me to what I came here to ask you. Briefly, my suggestion is that — if you felt equal to it and would care to — how about coming back here for a while? You look pretty fit, and, of course, you know all the ropes. I don't mean a lot of hard work for you — you need n't take anything strenuously — just a few odd jobs here and there, as you choose. What I'd like you for more than anything else is not for the actual work you'd do — though that, naturally, would be very valuable — but for your help in other ways — in just *belonging* here. There's nobody ever been more popular than you were, and are still — you'd help to hold things together if there were any danger of them flying to bits. And perhaps there *is* that danger. . . ."

Chips answered, breathlessly and with a holy joy in his heart: "I 'll come. . . ."

HE still kept on his rooms with Mrs. Wickett; indeed, he still lived there; but every morning, about half-past ten, he put on his coat and muffler and crossed the road to the School. He felt very fit, and the actual work was not taxing. Just a few forms in Latin and Roman History — the old lessons — even the old pronunciation. The same joke about the Lex Canuleia — there was a new generation that had not heard it, and he was absurdly gratified by the success it achieved. He felt a little like a music-hall favorite returning to the boards after a positively last appearance.

They all said how marvelous it was that he knew every boy's name and face so quickly. They did not guess how closely he had kept in touch from across the road.

He was a grand success altogether. In some strange way he did, and they all knew and felt it, help things. For the first time in his life he felt *necessary* — and necessary to something that was nearest his heart. There is no sublimer feeling in the world, and it was his at last.

He made new jokes, too — about the O.T.C. and the food-rationing system and the anti-air-raid blinds that had to be fitted on all the windows. There was a mysterious kind of rissole that began to appear on the School menu on Mondays, and Chips called it *abhorrendum* — "meat to be abhorred." The story went round — heard Chips's latest?

Chatteris fell ill during the winter of '17, and again, for the second time in his life, Chips became Acting Head of Brookfield. Then in April Chatteris died, and the Governors asked Chips if he would carry on "for the duration." He said he would, if they would refrain from appointing him officially. From that last honor, within his reach at last, he shrank instinctively, feeling himself in so many ways unequal to it. He said to Rivers: "You see, I'm not a young man and I don't want people to — um — expect a lot from me. I'm like all these new colonels and majors you see everywhere — just a war-time fluke. A ranker — that's all I am really."

1917. 1918. Chips lived through it all. He sat in the headmaster's study every morning, handling problems, dealing with plaints and requests. Out of vast experience had emerged a kindly, gentle confidence in himself. To keep

a sense of proportion, that was the main thing.
So much of the world was losing it; as well keep
it where it had, or ought to have, a congenial
home.

On Sundays in Chapel it was he who now
read out the tragic list, and sometimes it was seen
and heard that he was in tears over it. Well,
why not, the School said; he was an old man;
they might have despised anyone else for the
weakness.

One day he got a letter from Switzerland,
from friends there; it was heavily censored, but
conveyed some news. On the following Sunday,
after the names and biographies of old boys, he
paused a moment and then added: —

"Those few of you who were here before the
War will remember Max Staefel, the German
master. He was in Germany, visiting his home,
when war broke out. He was popular while he
was here, and made many friends. Those who

knew him will be sorry to hear that he was killed last week, on the Western Front."

He was a little pale when he sat down afterward, aware that he had done something unusual. He had consulted nobody about it, anyhow; no one else could be blamed. Later, outside the Chapel, he heard an argument: —

"On the Western Front, Chips said. Does that mean he was fighting for the Germans?"

"I suppose it does."

"Seems funny, then, to read his name out with all the others. After all, he was an *enemy*."

"Oh, just one of Chips's ideas, I expect. The old boy still has 'em."

Chips, in his room again, was not displeased by the comment. Yes, he still had 'em — those ideas of dignity and generosity that were becoming increasingly rare in a frantic world. And he thought: Brookfield will take them, too, from me; but it would n't from anyone else.

Once, asked for his opinion of bayonet practice being carried on near the cricket pavilion, he answered, with that lazy, slightly asthmatic intonation that had been so often and so extravagantly imitated: "It seems — to me — umph — a very vulgar way of killing people."

The yarn was passed on and joyously appreciated — how Chips had told some big brass hat from the War Office that bayonet fighting was vulgar. Just like Chips. And they found an adjective for him — an adjective just beginning to be used: he was pre-War.

And once, on a night of full moonlight, the air-raid warning was given while Chips was taking his lower fourth in Latin. The guns began almost instantly, and, as there was plenty of shrapnel falling about outside, it seemed to Chips that they might just as well stay where they were, on the ground floor of School House. It was pretty solidly built and made as good a dugout as Brookfield could offer; and as for a direct hit, well, they could not expect to survive that, wherever they were.

So he went on with his Latin, speaking a little louder amid the reverberating crashes of the guns and the shrill whine of anti-aircraft shells. Some of the boys were nervous; few were able to be attentive. He said, gently: "It may possibly seem to you, Robertson — at this particular moment in the world's history — umph — that the affairs of Cæsar in Gaul some two thousand years ago — are — umph — of somewhat secondary importance — and that — umph — the irregular conjugation of the verb *tollo* is — umph — even less important still. But believe me — umph — my dear Robertson — that is not really the case." Just then there came a particularly loud explosion — quite near. "You cannot — umph — judge the importance of things — umph — by the noise they make. Oh dear me, no." A little chuckle. "And these things — umph — that have mattered — for thousands of years — are not going to be — snuffed out — because some stink

105

merchant — in his laboratory — invents a new kind of mischief." Titters of nervous laughter; for Buffles, the pale, lean, and medically unfit science master, was nicknamed the Stink Merchant. Another explosion — nearer still. "Let us — um — resume our work. If it is fate that we are soon to be — umph — interrupted, let us be found employing ourselves in something — umph — really appropriate. Is there anyone who will volunteer to construe?"

Maynard, chubby, dauntless, clever, and impudent, said: "I will, sir."

"Very good. Turn to page forty and begin at the bottom line."

The explosions still continued deafeningly; the whole building shook as if it were being lifted off its foundations. Maynard found the page, which was some way ahead, and began, shrilly: —

"*Genus hoc erat pugnae* — this was the kind

106

of fight — *quo se Germani exercuerant* — in
which the Germans busied themselves. Oh, sir,
that's good -- that's really very funny indeed,
sir — one of your very best — "

Laughing began, and Chips added: "Well —
umph — you can see — now — that these dead
languages — umph — can come to life again —
sometimes — eh? Eh?"

Afterward they learned that five bombs had
fallen in and around Brookfield, the nearest of
them just outside the School grounds. Nine per-
sons had been killed.

The story was told, retold, embellished. "The
dear old boy never turned a hair. Even found
some old tag to illustrate what was going on.
Something in Cæsar about the way the Germans fought. You wouldn't think there were
things like that in Cæsar, would you? And the
way Chips laughed . . . you know the way he
does laugh . . . the tears all running down his

face . . . never seen him laugh so much. . . ."

He was a legend.

With his old and tattered gown, his walk that was just beginning to break into a stumble, his mild eyes peering over the steel-rimmed spectacles, and his quaintly humorous sayings, Brookfield would not have had an atom of him different.

November 11, 1918.

News came through in the morning; a whole holiday was decreed for the School, and the kitchen staff were implored to provide as cheerful a spread as war-time rationing permitted. There was much cheering and singing, and a bread fight across the Dining Hall. When Chips entered in the midst of the uproar there was an instant hush, and then wave upon wave of cheering; everyone gazed on him with eager, shining eyes, as on a symbol of victory. He walked to the dais, seeming as if he wished to speak; they made silence for him, but he shook his head after a moment, smiled, and walked away again.

It had been a damp, foggy day, and the walk across the quadrangle to the Dining Hall had given him a chill. The next day he was in bed with bronchitis, and stayed there till after Christmas. But already, on that night of November 11, after his visit to the Dining Hall, he had sent in his resignation to the Board of Governors.

When school reassembled after the holidays he was back at Mrs. Wickett's. At his own request there were no more farewells or presentations, nothing but a handshake with his successor and the word "acting" crossed out on official stationery. The "duration" was over.

And now, fifteen years after that, he could look back upon it all with a deep and sumptuous tranquillity. He was not ill, of course—only a little tired at times, and bad with his breathing during the winter months. He would not go abroad—he had once tried it, but had chanced to strike the Riviera during one of its carefully unadvertised cold spells. "I prefer—um—to get my chills—umph—in my own country," he used to say, after that. He had to take care of himself when there were east winds, but autumn and winter were not really so bad; there were warm fires, and books, and you could look forward to the summer. It was the summer that he liked best, of course; apart from the weather, which suited him, there were the continual visits of old boys. Every week-end some of them motored up to Brookfield and called at his house. Sometimes they tired him, if too many came at once; but he did not really mind; he could always rest and sleep afterward. And he enjoyed their visits — more than anything else in the world that was still to be enjoyed. "Well, Gregson — umph — I remember you — umph — always late for everything — eh — eh? Perhaps you'll be late in growing old — umph — like me — umph — eh?" And later, when he was alone again and Mrs. Wickett came in to clear away the tea things: "Mrs. Wickett, young Gregson called — umph — you remember him, do you?

Tall boy with spectacles. Always late. Umph. Got a job with the — umph — League of Nations — where — I suppose — his — um — dilatoriness — won't be noticeable — eh?"

And sometimes, when the bell rang for call-over, he would go to the window and look across the road and over the School fence and see, in the distance, the thin line of boys filing past the bench. New times, new names . . . but the old ones still remained . . . Jefferson, Jennings, Jolyon, Jupp, Kingsley Primus, Kingsley Secundus, Kingsley Tertius, Kingston . . . where are you all, where have you all gone to? . . . Mrs. Wickett, bring me a cup of tea just before prep, will you, please?

The post-War decade swept through with a clatter of change and maladjustments; Chips, as he lived through it, was profoundly disappointed when he looked abroad. The Ruhr, Chanak, Corfu; there was enough to be uneasy about in the world. But near him, at Brookfield, and even, in a wider sense, in England, there was something that charmed his heart because it was old — and had survived. More and more he saw the rest of the world as a vast disarrangement for which England had sacrificed enough — and perhaps too much. But he was satisfied with Brookfield. It was rooted in things that had stood the test of time and change and war. Curious, in this deeper sense, how little it *had* changed. Boys were a politer race; bullying was nonexistent; there was more swearing and cheating. There was a more genuine friendliness between master and boy — less pomposity on the one side, less unctuousness on the other. One of the new masters, fresh from Oxford, even let the Sixth call him by his Christian name. Chips did n't hold with that; indeed, he was just a little bit shocked. "He might as well — umph — sign his terminal reports — umph — 'yours affectionately' — eh — eh?" he told somebody.

During the General Strike of 1926, Brookfield boys loaded motor vans with foodstuffs. When it was all over, Chips felt stirred emotionally as he had not been since the War. Something had happened, something whose ultimate significance had yet to be reckoned. But one thing was clear: England had burned her fire in her own grate again. And when, at a Speech Day function that year, an American visitor laid stress on the vast sums that the strike had cost the country, Chips answered: "Yes, but — umph — advertisement — always *is* costly."

"Advertisement?"

"Well, was n't it — umph — advertisement — and very fine advertisement — too? A whole week of it — umph — and not a life lost — not a shot fired! Your country would have — umph — spilt more blood in — umph — raiding a single liquor saloon!"

Laughter . . . laughter . . . wherever he went and whatever he said, there was laughter. He had earned the reputation of being a great jester, and jests were expected of him. Whenever he rose to speak at a meeting, or even when he talked across a table, people prepared their minds and faces for the joke. They listened in a mood to be amused and it was easy to satisfy them. They laughed sometimes before he came to the point. "Old Chips was in fine form," they would say, afterward. "Marvelous the way he can always see the funny side of things. . . ."

After 1929, Chips did not leave Brookfield — even for Old Boys' dinners in London. He was afraid of chills, and late nights began to tire him too much. He came across to the School, however, on fine days; and he still kept up a wide and continual hospitality in his room. His faculties were all unimpaired, and he had no personal worries of any kind. His income was more than he needed to spend, and his small capital, invested in gilt-edged stocks, did not suffer when the slump set in. He gave a lot of money away — to people who called on him with a hard-luck story, to various School funds, and also to the Brookfield mission. In 1930 he made his will. Except for legacies to the mission and to Mrs. Wickett, he left all he had to found an open scholarship to the school.

1931. . . . 1932. . . .

"What do you think of Hoover, sir?"

"Do you think we shall ever go back to gold?"

"How d' you feel about things in general, sir? See any break in the clouds?"

"When 's the tide going to turn, Chips, old boy? You ought to know, with all your experience of things."

They all asked him questions, as if he were some kind of prophet and encyclopædia combined

—more even than that, for they liked their answer dished up as a joke. He would say: —

"Well, Henderson, when I was — umph — a much younger man — there used to be someone who — um — promised people ninepence for fourpence. I don't know that anybody — umph — ever got it, but — umph — our present rulers seem — um — to have solved the problem how to give — umph — fourpence for ninepence."

Laughter.

Sometimes, when he was strolling about the School, small boys of the cheekier kind would ask him questions, merely for the fun of getting Chips's "latest" to retail.

"Please, sir, what about the Five-Year Plan?"

"Sir, do you think Germany wants to fight another war?"

"Have you been to the new cinema, sir? I went with my people the other day. Quite a grand affair for a small place like Brookfield. They 've got a Wurlitzer."

"And what — umph — on earth — is a Wurlitzer?"

"It 's an organ, sir — a cinema organ."

"Dear me. . . . I 've seen the name on the hoardings, but I always — umph — imagined — it must be some kind of — umph — sausage."

Laughter. . . . Oh, there 's a new Chips joke, you fellows, a perfectly lovely one. I was gassing to the old boy about the new cinema, and . . .

He sat in his front parlor at Mrs. Wickett's on a November afternoon in thirty-three. It was cold and foggy, and he dared not go out. He had not felt too well since Armistice Day; he fancied he might have caught a slight chill during the Chapel service. Merivale had been that morning for his usual fortnightly chat. "Every-thing all right? Feeling hearty? That's the style — keep indoors this weather — there's a lot of flu about. Wish I could have your life for a day or two."

His life . . . and what a life it had been! The whole pageant of it swung before him as he sat by the fire that afternoon. The things he had done and seen: Cambridge in the sixties; Great Gable on an August morning; Brookfield at all times and seasons throughout the years. And, for that matter, the things he had *not* done, and would never do now that he had left them too late — he had never traveled by air, for instance, and he had never been to a talkie-show. So that he was both more and less experienced than the youngest new boy at the School might well be; and that, that paradox of age and youth, was what the world called progress.

Mrs. Wickett had gone out, visiting relatives in a neighboring village; she had left the tea things ready on the table, with bread and butter and extra cups laid out in case anybody called.

On such a day, however, visitors were not very likely; with the fog thickening hourly outside, he would probably be alone.

But no. About a quarter to four a ring came, and Chips, answering the front door himself (which he ought n't to have done), encountered a rather small boy wearing a Brookfield cap and an expression of anxious timidity. "Please, sir," he began, "does Mr. Chips live here?"

"Umph — you 'd better come inside," Chips answered. And in his room a moment later he added: "I am — umph — the person you want. Now what can I — umph — do for you?"

"I was told you wanted me, sir."

Chips smiled. An old joke — an old leg-pull, and he, of all people, having made so many old jokes in his time, ought not to complain. And it amused him to cap their joke, as it were, with one of his own; to let them see that he could keep his end up, even yet. So he said, with eyes

twinkling: "Quite right, my boy. I wanted you
to take tea with me. Will you — umph — sit
down by the fire? Umph — I don't think I have
seen your face before. How is that?"

"I've only just come out of the sanatorium,
sir — I've been there since the beginning of term
with measles."

"Ah, that accounts for it."

Chips began his usual ritualistic blending of
tea from the different caddies; luckily there was
half a walnut cake with pink icing in the cup-
board. He found out that the boy's name was
Linford, that he lived in Shropshire, and that
he was the first of his family at Brookfield.

"You know — umph — Linford — you'll like
Brookfield — when you get used to it. It's not
half such an awful place — as you imagine.
You're a bit afraid of it — um, yes — eh? So
was I, my dear boy — at first. But that was —
um — a long time ago. Sixty-three years ago —

umph — to be precise. When I — um — first went into Big Hall and — um — I saw all those boys — I tell you — I was quite scared. Indeed — umph — I don't tnink I've ever been so scared in my life. Not even when — umph — the Germans bombed us — during the War. But — umph — it did n't last long — the scared feeling, I mean. I soon made myself — um — at home."

"Were there a lot of other new boys that term, sir?" asked Linford shyly.

"Eh? But — God bless my soul — I was n't a boy at all — I was a man — a young man of twenty-two! And the next time you see a young man — a new master — taking his first prep in Big Hall — umph — just think — what it feels like!"

"But if you were twenty-two then, sir —"

"Yes? Eh?"

"You must be — very old — now, sir."

Chips laughed quietly and steadily to himself. It was a good joke.

"Well — umph — I 'm certainly — umph — no chicken."

He laughed quietly to himself for a long time. Then he talked of other matters, of Shropshire, of schools and school life in general, of the news in that day's papers. "You 're growing up into — umph — a very cross sort of world, Linford. Maybe it will have got over some of its — umph — crossness — by the time you 're ready for it. Let's hope so — umph — at any rate. . . . Well . . ." And with a glance at the clock he delivered himself of his old familiar formula. "I 'm — umph — sorry — you can't stay . . ."

At the front door he shook hands.

"Good-bye, my boy."

And the answer came, in a shrill treble: "Good-bye, Mr. Chips. . . ."

Chips sat by the fire again, with those words echoing along the corridors of his mind. "Good-bye, Mr. Chips. . . ." An old leg-pull, to make new boys think that his name was really Chips; the joke was almost traditional. He did not mind. "Good-bye, Mr. Chips. . . ." He remembered that on the eve of his wedding day Kathie had used that same phrase, mocking him gently for the seriousness he had had in those days. He thought: Nobody would call me serious to-day, that's very certain. . . .

Suddenly the tears began to roll down his cheeks — an old man's failing; silly, perhaps, but he couldn't help it. He felt very tired; talking to Linford like that had quite exhausted him. But he was glad he had met Linford. Nice boy. Would do well.

Over the fog-laden air came the bell for callover, tremulous and muffled. Chips looked at the window, graying into twilight; it was time to light up. But as soon as he began to move he felt that he could n't; he was too tired; and, anyhow, it did n't matter. He leaned back in his chair. No chicken — eh, well — that was true enough. And it had been amusing about Linford. A neat score off the jokers who had sent the boy over. Good-bye, Mr. Chips . . . odd, though, that he should have said it just like that. . . .

WHEN he awoke, for he seemed to have been asleep, he found himself in bed; and Merivale was there, stooping over him and smiling. "Well, you old ruffian — feeling all right? That was a fine shock you gave us!"

Chips murmured, after a pause, and in a voice that surprised him by its weakness: "Why — um — what — what has happened?"

"Merely that you threw a faint. Mrs. Wickett came in and found you — lucky she did. You 're all right now. 'Take it easy. Sleep again if you feel inclined."

He was glad someone had suggested such a good idea. He felt so weak that he was n't even puzzled by the details of the business — how they had got him upstairs, what Mrs. Wickett had said, and so on. But then, suddenly, at the other side of the bed, he saw Mrs. Wickett. She was smiling. He thought: God bless my soul, what 's she doing up here? And then, in the shadows behind Merivale, he saw Cartwright, the new Head (he thought of him as "new," even though he had been at Brookfield since 1919), and old Buffles, commonly called "Roddy." Funny, the way they were all here. He felt: Anyhow, I can't be bothered to wonder why about anything. I 'm going to go to sleep.

But it was n't sleep, and it was n't quite wakefulness, either; it was a sort of in-between state, full of dreams and faces and voices. Old scenes

and old scraps of tunes: a Mozart trio that Kathie
had once played in — cheers and laughter and
the sound of guns — and, over it all, Brookfield
bells, Brookfield bells. "So you see, if Miss Plebs
wanted Mr. Patrician to marry her . . . yes, you
can, you liar. . . ." Joke . . . Meat to be abhorred. . . . Joke . . . That you, Max? Yes,
come in. What's the news from the Father-
land? . . . *O mihi praeteritos* . . . Ralston said
I was slack and inefficient — but they couldn't
manage without me. . . . *Obile heres ago forti-
bus es in aro* . . . Can you translate that, any of
you? . . . It's a joke. . . .

Once he heard them talking about him in the
room.

Cartwright was whispering to Merivale. "Poor
old chap — must have lived a lonely sort of life,
all by himself."

Merivale answered: "Not always by himself.
He married, you know."

"Oh, did he? I never knew about that."

"She died. It must have been — oh, quite thirty years ago. More, possibly."

"Pity. Pity he never had any children."

And at that, Chips opened his eyes as wide as he could and sought to attract their attention. It was hard for him to speak out loud, but he managed to murmur something, and they all looked round and came nearer to him.

He struggled, slowly, with his words. "What — was that — um — you were saying — about me — just now?"

Old Buffles smiled and said: "Nothing at all, old chap — nothing at all — we were just wondering when you were going to wake out of your beauty sleep."

"But — umph — I heard you — you *were* talking about me — "

"Absolutely nothing of any consequence, my dear fellow — really, I give you my word. . . ."

130

"I thought I heard you — one of you — saying it was a pity — umph — a pity I never had — any children . . . eh? . . . But I have, you know . . . I have . . ."

The others smiled without answering, and after a pause Chips began a faint and palpitating chuckle.

"Yes — umph — I have," he added, with quavering merriment. "Thousands of 'em . . . thousands of 'em . . . and all boys."

And then the chorus sang in his ears in final harmony, more grandly and sweetly than he had ever heard it before, and more comfortingly too. . . . Pettifer, Pollett, Porson, Potts, Pullman, Purvis, Pym-Wilson, Radlett, Rapson, Reade, Reaper, Reddy Primus . . . come round me now, all of you, for a last word and a joke. . . . Harper, Haslett, Hatfield, Hatherley . . . my last joke . . . did you hear it? . . . Did it make you laugh? . . . Bone, Boston, Bovey, Bradford,

Bradley, Bramhall-Anderson . . . wherever you are, whatever has happened, give me this moment with you . . . this last moment . . . my boys . . .

And soon Chips was asleep.

He seemed so peaceful that they did not disturb him to say good-night; but in the morning, as the School bell sounded for breakfast, Brook-field had the news. "Brookfield will never forget his lovableness," said Cartwright, in a speech to the School. Which was absurd, because all things are forgotten in the end. But Linford, at any rate, will remember and tell the tale: "I said good-bye to Chips the night before he died. . . ."